To Sarah Elizabeth Jackson, who wanted to hear a story—C.C.

To Spencer, Jessie, and Ian and their splendid snozzbeakers—K.H.

Library of Congress Cataloging in Publication. Cowan, Catherine. The nose/by Nikolai Gogol; as retold for children by Catherine Cowan; illustrated by Kevin Hawkes. p. cm. Summary: After disappearing from the Deputy Inspector's face, his nose shows up around town before returning to its proper place. ISBN 0-688-10464-9.—ISBN 0-688-10465-7 (lib. bdg.) [1. Nose—Fiction.] I. Gogol', Nikolaĭ Vasil'evich, 1809–1852. Nos. II. Hawkes, Kevin, ill. III. Title. PZ7.C8347No 1995 [E]—dc 20 93-4975 CIP AC

The illustrations in this book were done in acrylic paints on 2 ply acid-free museum board. The display type was hand-lettered by Anthony Bloch. The text type was set in Perpetua by Miller & Debel. Color separations by Beaumont Graphics. Printed and bound by Berryville. Production supervision by Linda Palladino.

NIKOLAI GOGOL'S

The Nose

AS RETOLD FOR CHILDREN
BY CATHERINE COWAN
PAINTINGS BY KEVIN HAWKES

Lothrop, Lee & Shepard Books   New York

ANY, MANY YEARS AGO in a city far away, a barber named Ivan awoke one morning to the smell of hot bread fresh from the oven. When his wife set a loaf before him, he picked up a knife and cut it in half. To his surprise, there inside, right in the center, he saw something strange. He prodded it with a finger. It was solid.

He dug into the bread and pulled it out. It looked like a nose! He rubbed his eyes and looked again. Yes, it *was* a nose—and a familiar one, too.

When his wife saw the nose, she shrieked, "Oh, my! What *have* you done?"

Ivan scratched behind his ear. Am I dreaming? he wondered. Otherwise, how could this be? Bread is one thing, and a nose, quite another.

"I'm going straight to the police," announced his wife. "Why, you've either yanked or cut off some gentleman's nose."

The poor man was in shock. He recognized the nose. It belonged to a Deputy Inspector of Reindeer whom he shaved twice a week. He started to wrap it up and put it in a corner, but his wife kept yelling at him.

Poor Ivan was so flustered, he didn't know what to do. At last, he wadded the nose in a rag and fled to the street.

He wanted to get rid of it, to shove it under something or drop it as if by accident and quickly walk away. But he kept meeting people he knew. Suddenly, he had an idea and hurried off to a bridge over the river.

When he got there, he looked around cautiously. Then, leaning over the railing as though looking for fish, he let the rag slip from his hand.

He was feeling quite smug…until a policeman beckoned.

Meanwhile, in another part of the city, the Deputy Inspector of Reindeer awoke. He yawned and stretched and thought about many things. Then he remembered that the night before, he had discovered a spot on his nose.

Deciding to check if the spot was still there, he looked in the mirror. To his surprise, he saw no spot. In fact, he saw no nose! What he saw was a totally empty flat place where his nose should have been.

He pinched himself and rubbed his eyes with a towel. But his nose was *not* there. Someone had stolen it!

He quickly dressed and, with a handkerchief clutched to his face, rushed off to report his missing nose to the police.

However, the more he thought about it, the more impossible it seemed. Who ever heard of losing a nose? Then he glanced in a pastry shop window and uncovered his face. Nothing! He felt the place. It was perfectly smooth.

As he hurried on down the street, he was stopped in his tracks when a carriage drew up before him. A gentleman jumped down and rushed inside a house.

Only this was no ordinary gentleman. It was his nose. The poor man nearly fainted away.

Before long, the nose came out again, climbed back into the carriage, and rode off down the street. And what a proud nose it was! It was dressed in a gold-embroidered uniform, a hat with a plume, and a sword at its side. Why, it was dressed as a Grand and Glorious Governor of Games, a rank of importance indeed.

The Deputy Inspector thought he must be going out of his mind. What was he to make of a nose, which only yesterday had known its place, now walking and driving about—and dressed in a uniform, too?

He raced after the carriage until it stopped before the cathedral, then, following the nose, he dashed up the steps and inside.

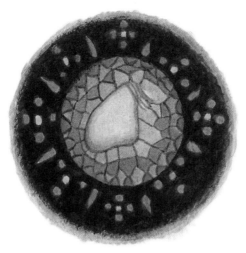

The nose stood apart from the other worshippers, saying its prayers with its face completely hidden by the large stand-up collar of its uniform. Hesitantly, the Deputy Inspector approached and cleared his throat. "Sir," he said.

The nose turned. "Yes, what is it you want?"

"E-excuse me, sir," he stammered, "but I-I believe you should know your place."

"I beg your pardon! Explain yourself," said the nose.

"Well, you see, sir, what with my position and all, I can't go about with no nose."

"What? I don't understand. Try to make yourself clear."

"Well, sir. I mean…well, it's perfectly clear. What I mean, sir, is this….You are my nose, and you really should know your place. And that, if you don't mind my saying, is here on my face."

"I believe you're mistaken," said the nose. "It should be obvious to anyone that I am myself. Besides, I see by your coat that there can be no connection between us. We don't even work in the same department. Your nose, indeed!" And saying this, the nose turned and walked away.

The Deputy Inspector hurried after, but when he reached the street, his nose was nowhere to be seen—not even the plume on its hat.

He wrung his hands and went first this way, then that.

At the newspaper office he tried placing an ad offering a reward for his nose, but the clerk there only shook his head. It was absurd. Who ever heard of losing one's nose? So the Deputy Inspector showed him the place.

"How unbelievably odd!" said the man. "The area is as flat as a pancake." Yet he refused the ad.

Next the Deputy Inspector went to report his loss to the police, but everyone there was too busy to pay any attention.

Returning home late in the day, he went to the mirror and squinched up his eyes, hoping to surprise his nose back where it should be. But alas, it was not there.

Had he lost a button, a spoon, or even his watch, that would have been different. But to lose his nose! It was simply impossible, too silly for words. He was sure his nose had been there only the day before. Now it was going about the city paying calls, and dressed in a uniform, too.

Still lost in thought, the Deputy Inspector heard a voice in the hall asking for him. He jumped up and rushed to the door.

There in the hallway stood a policeman.

"Excuse me, sir. Did you lose your nose?" the policeman asked.

"Yes! I fear I did," he answered.

"Well, it's been found, sir. It was intercepted trying to leave town. Funny thing is, I first mistook him—it, that is, sir—for a Grand and Glorious Governor of Games. Luckily I was wearing my glasses at the time, and I saw right away that it was only a nose."

The Deputy Inspector was so excited, he asked for it at once. The policeman handed him his nose, explaining that somehow his barber, whom he had suspected for a long time of stealing buttons from a shop, was involved.

But the Deputy Inspector heard not a word. He cupped the nose in his hands, sputtering, "Yes, oh yes, this is my nose."

After the policeman had gone, the Deputy Inspector looked his nose over. Yes, there was the spot he remembered, where it had been only the night before. He almost giggled with delight. Then, slowly and carefully so as not to get it on crooked, he placed it back on his face. But to his horror, it immediately fell off.

He warmed his nose. He breathed on it. He licked it. But still it would not stick. Though he scolded it soundly—"Come on! Stay on, you dummy! Stick!"—the nose refused to. Finally, he sent for a doctor.

"Yes, I could stitch it on," said the doctor, "but that might turn out worse. No, if I were you, I would leave well enough alone."

"But this is *not* well enough," cried the Deputy Inspector. "I want my nose back again. Right here where it belongs."

"I'm sorry, but you must simply leave it up to nature. If you wish to keep it, wash it every day or, better, put it in a bottle of vinegar. However, should you decide to sell it, I might be interested."

"Never!" cried the Deputy Inspector. "I'd rather it rotted away!"

"Ah, well," said the doctor, and he left.

One morning not long after, the nose appeared, just as if nothing had happened, in the middle of the Deputy Inspector's face. With a joyous shout, he leaped about the room. Again and again he glanced in the mirror to see that his nose was still there.

First he checked with this person, then that, saying, "Do you see a spot on my nose?" He hardly dared to breathe for fear that they would see neither a spot nor a nose. But everyone saw exactly what he did: no spot, but a nose.

And so the nose returned without so much as a word of explanation.

That same morning, Ivan came to shave the Deputy Inspector. The barber draped him with a cloth and lathered his chin and cheeks while studying the nose. So! It was back. How very strange! He raised two fingers to gently grasp the tip.

"Mind what you're doing there!" snapped the Deputy Inspector.

Then, ever so carefully, though he found it most awkward, Ivan managed to shave him without a single cut or even once yanking his nose.

After that, rumors flew about the city concerning a certain nose which had just been seen driving about in this park or shopping in that shop. But none of them were true. From that time on, the nose only ventured out right where it belonged—in the middle of the Deputy Inspector's face.